DISNEY PRINCESS
BEGINNINGS

ARIEL
Makes Waves

BY LIZ MARSHAM

ILLUSTRATED BY
THE DISNEY STORYBOOK ART TEAM

Random House 🏠 New York

For Nachie—

we have all the best adventures.

—L.M.

Published in
the United States by Random House Children's Books, a division of Penguin
Random House LLC, 1745 Broadway, New York, NY 10019, and in Canada by
Penguin Random House Canada Limited, Toronto, in conjunction with Disney
Enterprises, Inc. Random House and the colophon are registered trademarks of
Penguin Random House LLC.
randomhousekids.com

Library of Congress Cataloging-in-Publication Data
Names: Marsham, Liz, author. | Disney Storybook Art Team, illustrator.
Title: Ariel makes waves / Liz Marsham ; illustrated by the Disney Storybook
Art Team.
Description: New York : Random House, [2017] | Series: Disney princess
beginnings ; 3
Identifiers: LCCN 2016041415 | ISBN 978-0-7364-3733-2 (paperback) |
ISBN 978-0-7364-8196-0 (lib. bdg.)
Subjects: | BISAC: JUVENILE FICTION / Media Tie-In. | JUVENILE
FICTION / Action & Adventure / General.
Classification: LCC PZ7.1.M37295 Ar 2017 | DDC [E]—dc23

Printed in the United States of America
10 9 8 7

Book design by Jenna Huerta & Betty Avila

This book has been officially leveled by using the F&P Text Level Gradient™
Leveling System.

Chapter 1
Out of the Reef

"*A*riel, catch up!"

Ariel blinked in surprise. Just a minute ago she and her six older sisters had been getting ready to go to breakfast, and then she had gotten distracted by the new sea sponges outside their bedroom window.

They were bright red, almost the exact shade of her hair. *Where did they come from?* she wondered. She knew the royal gardeners had placed them there, but she couldn't remember seeing sponges like these on the nearby coral reef. Maybe one day, when she was older, she could—

"Ariel!"

She turned toward the voice. Five of her sisters were already gone! Attina, the oldest, floated by the door, flipping her tail impatiently. *Ugh,* Ariel thought, *now Attina's going to want to swim her fastest to catch up with everyone.* But Attina was thirteen and Ariel was only seven, so of course Ariel's tail was smaller, meaning she couldn't swim as fast. This happened all the time.

Just yesterday—

"Ariel!"

Ariel's eyes snapped back to her sister, who was swimming toward her, a determined look on her face. *Uh-oh.* Attina took Ariel by the shoulder and swirled her around to face the mirror, then began working a brush through Ariel's long red hair. "Is your bandeau clean, at least?" Attina asked.

Feeling self-conscious, Ariel looked down. She was wearing her favorite top today: simple and purple. She'd picked it out herself. And, yes, it was clean. She touched the strip of cloth and nodded, then winced as the motion made the brush catch in her hair.

"Good. All done," Attina announced. Ariel faced her sister for inspection. While Attina looked her over, Ariel's gaze drifted to Attina's auburn hair, perfectly done up as always, and her five-pointed tiara, perfectly in place as always. Attina nodded in satisfaction and motioned toward the door. *She's so confident,* Ariel thought as she started swimming. *When will I feel like that?*

When they arrived in the palace dining room, breakfast was over. Ariel's father, King

Triton, shook his head when she arrived late, but luckily he was too busy today to scold her properly. With a quick "Listen to your sisters, Ariel," he swam off with his advisers to attend to the business of ruling Atlantica.

Ariel didn't even get the chance to ask him if he could come out with them. Every day the sisters had time after breakfast to play on the reef. Ariel always invited the king along, and sometimes he said yes. Those were the best days. Ariel was trying to figure out the pattern: Did he say yes more often on days when he had an extra kelp cake? Or was he more likely to be agreeable on the days when she wore a flower in her hair? Or maybe —

"Ariel!"

She looked up from her empty plate. Her sisters were heading for the archway that led to the palace exit, looking back over their shoulders at her. Andrina was swimming toward Ariel.

"You know, if you like that plate so much, you can take it with you. We've got more." Andrina kept her face serious, but Ariel knew she was teasing.

"No, it's not that. The plate, I mean. I was thinking . . ." Ariel always felt a little flustered when Andrina joked with her.

Andrina flopped down in the chair next to Ariel, pushing her short blond hair out of her eyes and sinking her chin into her hands in a listening pose. By the archway, the five older sisters made impatient noises. "Go on! We'll catch up!" Andrina called to them.

"We *can't* go without you, and you know

it!" Alana, the second oldest, called back. She was twelve. "You're both too little!"

Andrina turned to Ariel and rolled her eyes, which made Ariel giggle and relax a bit. "Okay, little sis. We don't have much time. What's your worry in ten words or less?"

Ten words weren't nearly enough to explain herself! Ariel tried her best. "I want Daddy to play with us more. Kelp cakes?"

Andrina snorted with laughter. "Try again."

Ariel furrowed her brow. "If Daddy eats more kelp cakes, will he play with us more?"

This time Andrina ticked off the words on her fingers. "Hmm, we'll call that close enough." She seemed to understand what Ariel was asking. "No, silly head. Daddy plays with us whenever he can take a break from running the kingdom, and that's all there is to it. He wouldn't let something like kelp cakes make that decision."

Ariel slumped down in her seat. Of course Andrina was right. But that made Ariel's plan to get the royal cooks to make more kelp cakes kind of pointless, since—

Andrina grabbed Ariel's hand and pulled her away from the table. "Now that we've got *that* figured out, let's go! Remember, we're playing Ride the Current today!"

Ariel looked over at Andrina as they

swam toward the arch together. *She's only one year older than I am, but she thinks so fast, and sometimes she just seems to know so much,* Ariel thought. *When will I be like that?*

"Ariel, catch up!" yelled Aquata.

Out on the reef, the three oldest sisters — Attina, Alana, and eleven-year-old Adella — relaxed among the coral, gossiping and doing one another's hair. Once in a while they would glance over at the other four to call out instructions or make jokes.

The four younger sisters swam above them,

playing Ride the Current. Ariel was excited and nervous, since she had just started playing the game a few months ago. The current that ran over the coral reef could go very fast, and her sisters had only recently decided she was strong enough to swim out of it before getting carried too far away. The first time she'd played, Ariel worried that maybe she *wasn't* strong enough. *But I was fine in the end,* she reminded herself. *I was stronger than I thought I—*

"Ariel! Come on. Catch up!"

She looked around. The other three had already swum into the current! Ten-year-old Aquata was waving at her, beckoning her to hurry up. Ariel propelled herself into the fast-moving stream of water, letting out a *whee!* as she was whooshed away after them.

When she swam free of the current and tumbled back into slow-moving waters, Andrina and Aquata were waiting for her, along with nine-year-old Arista. Aquata was peering at her skeptically.

Ariel looked down at herself. "What? What's wrong?"

"I think I just figured out how you can swim a bit faster," Aquata said. "You've got to glide into it." She turned around and lifted up her long brown hair so Ariel could see her whole back. "Like this." She flexed her shoulders and back, then continued the motion through to a powerful whap of her tail. "Now you try."

Ariel tried to copy her, arching her back gracefully and then whipping her tail, but something went wrong and she ended up twisted around and upside down. Her three sisters burst out laughing, and after a moment Ariel did, too.

Aquata reached out and pulled Ariel right side up again. "You'll get it," she said. "Just keep practicing. In the meantime, ready to ride that current again?"

Ariel nodded, and the four girls headed upstream. Ariel watched Aquata swim powerfully through the water. *She's so strong,* Ariel thought. *Sometimes I can't see how I'll ever be like that, even with all the practice in the world. When did she practice? I wonder if—*

"Arieeeeel!" her three sisters chorused. Lost in thought, Ariel had fallen behind again. With a sigh, she flipped her tail as hard as she could and tried her best to catch up.

Chapter 2
Whisked Away

"All right," Attina called as the girls swam back after another exciting ride. "One more, and then it's time to head home!"

Ariel shook her head. "I can't believe it! It feels like we just got here a few minutes ago!"

"What do you mean, 'a few minutes'?" Arista said, and giggled. "We've ridden that current so many times, I'm dizzy just thinking about it! You girls can go for one last spin if

you want, but I'm going to put my fins up."
She swam toward the reef, shouting, "Alana,
scooch over so I can lie down! This tail is
tired!"

Raising an eyebrow, Andrina muttered,
"That tail doesn't *sound* tired."

Aquata laughed and held out her hands
to Ariel and Andrina. "Okay, just the three
of us, then. Want to hold hands this time?"

Ariel and Andrina nodded and grabbed
Aquata's hands. Together the girls counted,
"One . . . two . . . *three!*" and flung themselves
into the current.

"Wheeee!" yelled Ariel as they were
whisked away again. But a second later she

noticed something new. Much colder water trickled by her cheek, then by her arm, then by her stomach, until . . .

"Brrr!" Aquata shivered. "Feels like another current is joining this one, and it's freezing! Let's get out!"

Still holding hands, the three girls tried to move toward the slower water, but to their surprise, they were still caught in the current. They swam harder, but the stream held them fast. The current was getting colder and stronger!

"Let's try again," Aquata said, frowning. "One . . . two . . . *three!*"

The girls whipped their tails as hard as they could, but it was no use. They were stuck in the current and getting farther away from their home by the second.

"Maybe if I let go of your hand—" Andrina started to say, but Aquata cut her off with a sharp *"No!"* Ariel felt Aquata grip her hand harder.

It's all right, Ariel thought. *Aquata will figure this out.* "So what should we do?" she asked.

"I'm the strongest, so I can try to pull us all out," Aquata said. "Andrina, get over here! Both of you, grab on and stay as close to me as you can!"

Aquata pulled the two in, and Andrina and Ariel wrapped their arms around Aquata's shoulders and back. Aquata put her head down and threw her whole body to the right, trying with powerful strokes of her tail to break free of the rushing water.

Andrina looked back over her shoulder. "There goes the reef," she said.

Startled, Ariel looked back as well. Andrina was right! The familiar reef was shrinking into the distance, and strange rock formations now covered the seafloor below them. *Oh no,* Ariel thought. *We're going to be in a lot of trouble when we get back.*

"Keep . . . your heads . . . down!" Aquata said, panting. "There's less . . . drag . . . that way."

Ariel and Andrina obediently ducked their heads. *It feels like we're making*

progress, Ariel thought. *So why isn't the water slowing down?*

They broke apart to look at their surroundings. "Uh," Andrina said, "I hate to say this, but I think the current got a lot wider."

"How wide can a current get?" Ariel asked in alarm.

Andrina stared blankly back at her. "As wide as this, I guess?"

"Not . . . helping!" Aquata growled, still swimming her hardest.

"But this doesn't feel like a current anymore," continued Andrina. "It feels like some kind of—"

"Rogue wave!" hundreds of tiny voices

screeched from behind them. The girls cringed as a huge school of anchovies began streaming past on all sides. "Rogue wave!"

"Yikes!" Andrina yelped, shrinking closer to Aquata's back.

Ariel poked her head up. "What's a rogue wave?" she shouted to the fish. Then she felt foolish. *Which one am I even talking to?* she wondered. *By the time one of them hears me, they'll be too far ahead to answer.*

To her surprise, small groups of the anchovies began to respond.

"Currents . . . ," shrilled one group, flying past on her left.

"Can combine . . . ," trilled another group on her right. Ariel turned her head to find them, but they were gone.

"Get stronger . . ." A third group had managed to swim level with Ariel for a moment, fastening their tiny eyes on her. "And then . . ."

The whole school took up the shout: "Rogue waaaaaave!" The whirling mass of fish continued to swirl around the three mermaids as Aquata fought to swim at an angle to the rushing current. Soon the last few stragglers whooshed by, peeping *"Rogue wave! Rogue wave!"* as they went.

Then Aquata began coughing. Ariel looked down at her sister and immediately saw why: a surge of muddy water was rushing up and surrounding them!

"Oh, great," Andrina said, groaning. "The wave is stirring up the seafloor. This is all we—"

"Wait!" Ariel interrupted. "Are we slowing down?"

They *were* slowing down! Aquata continued to swim as hard as she could, but the current was no longer tugging on them as strongly.

"Aquata!" Ariel cheered. "You did it! You"—*cough*—"got us out!"

Aquata gave one last flip of her tail, which finally pushed the sisters into peaceful water. But just then a cloud of ooze came up around them.

The three girls hugged one another tightly.

"Aquata? What should"—*cough*—"we do now?" Ariel asked.

There was no answer except Aquata's coughing.

"Andrina?"

"I'm out of ideas" — *cough* — "little sis."

Ariel peered into the muddy water that surrounded them. She couldn't see a thing. They were all alone; they were lost. Aquata was exhausted, and Andrina was out of ideas.

Who was going to get them out of this?

Chapter 3
To the Light

riel realized she was wrong. She could see *one* thing: sunlight. It was filtering through the mud from above. She had an idea. They should swim up!

She caught Aquata's eye and pointed upward. Aquata just looked back at her, confused. Next Ariel looked to Andrina, but Andrina had her face tucked into Aquata's neck and was mumbling to herself. Ariel leaned in close to hear.

"And next we'll probably get eaten by a shark. The muck will probably annoy a shark. And then the shark will find us and think"— *cough, cough*—"'My day is looking up!' and then . . ."

Anxiously, Ariel pulled back. A stray thought popped into her mind: *Maybe I should be panicking, too?* She tried to push the thought away, but then she hesitated. *How do I know my idea is any good? If it were any good, wouldn't they have thought of it?*

No, this was the right thing to do. She knew it.

Ariel grabbed Aquata's and Andrina's hands and swam upward, tugging them along. When she looked down, she saw them both staring at her, wide-eyed and unsure. She nodded vigorously, turned her face toward the sun, and kept tugging.

Eventually, her sisters stopped resisting and followed Ariel. The three rose higher and higher through the muddy waters. Ahead of them, things looked clearer.

I did it! Ariel thought. *I did—*

And then her head broke the surface of the water and she was breathing in air. The warm sun winked off the gentle waves rising and falling around her. A short distance

away was a tiny island, hardly more than a pile of rocks. She barely had time to take it all in before Andrina and Aquata splashed up on either side of her.

Andrina's jaw dropped. "Oh boy," she said.

Sputtering, Aquata pressed her hand to her forehead. "Oh no, Ariel. Oh no. What did you do? We are not supposed to be here! Daddy is going to kill us!"

Ariel shrugged. "I didn't know how close we were. The wave must have brought us into shallow waters. But at least we can see where we are, right?"

Aquata stared at her. "Ariel! 'Where we are' is *on the surface*!"

For a moment Ariel thought about the rules she and her sisters were breaking. King Triton had told them over and over: no going to the surface and no contact with humans. *Ever.* But on the other hand, they had needed to escape the muddy water, and she had made a decision. She had been confident, just like Attina, and it had worked. And anyway, there were no humans in sight. For the first time since the current had turned cold and their day had been turned upside down, Ariel started to relax.

She raised her face to the sun and smiled. "Isn't this nice?" she said.

Chapter 4
Friendly Creatures

Ariel started making her way toward the small cluster of rocks. She thought she could hear something. . . .

"Ariel! Where are you going *now*?" Aquata called behind her.

Ariel turned around. "Well, I was thinking. We can't just dive right back down, can we?"

"No, please, no," Andrina said. "I'm still getting the muck out of my ears!"

Ariel looked over at Aquata. "And you need a break from swimming."

Aquata's shoulders slumped. "Yeah."

"So," Ariel continued, "if we head over to those rocks, we can get some rest. Maybe the mud will settle down. Then we can swim home in clearer water."

Andrina and Aquata looked at her in surprise.

"Uh . . . unless you think that's a bad p-plan?" Ariel stammered.

"No," Aquata said. "That makes a lot of sense. But, Ariel, aren't you . . ."

"What?" Ariel asked.

"Aren't you nervous about being up here?"

Ariel thought for a moment. *It seems all right so far. . . . Did I miss something?*

"I don't think so. Are you?"

Aquata blinked and then straightened her back. "Um, no! Not at all! Let's head for those rocks already." She swam past Ariel and toward the island without waiting for a reply.

"I'm impressed, little sis," Andrina said with a wink as she swam after Aquata.

Ariel trailed behind them, so pleased and distracted by the unexpected praise that she almost crashed into them when they stopped dead.

"What's wr—?" she started to ask.

But Andrina clapped a hand over Ariel's mouth to shush her. "Listen," she whispered.

Ariel listened. A faint noise was coming from the direction of the nearest rock. *Oh, right!* she thought. *I did hear something before!* Ariel pulled away from Andrina's hand. "Something's definitely alive on that rock, and it sounds . . . I don't know. It sounds . . ."

"It sounds awful!" Aquata fretted next to her.

"It sounds scary," whispered Andrina.

"No," Ariel said, surprising herself with how calm she felt. "It sounds sad. I'll go look."

Aquata grabbed for her, but Ariel was already too far away. She swam to the rock ledge, where the noise was coming from, and carefully pulled herself up, just enough to peek over.

In a puddle in the middle of the island was a white-and-gray . . . What was it? Whatever it was, it was little and wet and making the saddest noise, a high wailing that sounded a lot like crying. Ariel dropped back into the water and motioned for her sisters to come over. Aquata shook her head dramatically, so Ariel held up her hands just a little ways apart to show that the creature was small.

Curious, Andrina drifted forward a bit, and then looked back at Aquata. Aquata sighed and gave in, and the two of them joined Ariel. All at once, the three of them grabbed the rock ledge and pulled themselves up until they could see the strange creature. "It's a *bird*!" Andrina said breathlessly.

The creature stopped crying and whipped its head around to look at them.

"Eek! Humans!" it screeched.

"We are *not!*" Aquata said.

"It's okay!" Ariel jumped in. "We're not going to hurt you." She lifted herself up to sit on the rock and flipped her tail into view. "Look! We're mermaids!"

The little creature froze, staring at Ariel's tail. "Mermaids?"

"Yes, that's right," said Ariel. "And . . . you're a . . . bird?"

"I'm a seagull," the little bird said, relaxing a bit. "My name's Salty."

Ariel leaned in. "Nice to meet you, Salty. My—"

"*Ariel, stop!*" Aquata hissed. She and Andrina were still peeking over the ledge, only the tops of their heads and their eyes visible. "Don't get too close!"

"Yeah," Andrina agreed, "it's a little creepy."

"I can hear you!" Salty protested. "And I am not creepy!"

"No, you're not," said Ariel, shooting a glance at her sisters. "I'm Ariel, and these are my sisters Aquata and Andrina. We don't normally come to the surface, so we don't see many seagulls."

" 'Many'? You mean *any, ever*," Andrina muttered.

"Oh," Salty said, "then I guess you haven't seen my mother."

"Oh no!" Ariel cried. "Are you lost, too? What happened?"

"I don't really know," said the little seagull. "We were flying along over the water just like we always do, and then this huge wave came," he continued, talking faster and faster. "And I didn't get out of the way fast enough and it hit me and then I hit this rock and now it hurts and

I'm in a puddle and I don't know where my mom is and everything is bad!" His voice rose higher on the last word, and then he was crying again.

"Hey, hey, it's all right," Ariel said, trying to soothe him. She looked to her sisters for help, but they just stared back at her in confusion. Ariel took a deep breath. "Sometimes my problems come all at once, too," she told Salty. "My father tells me to take them one at a time."

Salty's crying petered out; he looked up at her. "What does that mean?"

"Well," Ariel said, "I know one problem we can fix. We can get you out of that puddle. Come here." She reached for the seagull and, ignoring her sisters' gasps, carefully picked him up and set him on a dry rock. "There you go."

Salty looked down at himself. "Oh yeah," he said. "I could have done that."

"Next," Ariel said, "where are you hurt?"

Salty shrugged. "Kind of all over."

Ariel heard a sigh from the ledge, and then Aquata hoisted herself up to sit next to Ariel. "All right, seagull. I can help with this one," she said. "Move one part of yourself at a time and see if it hurts. First do your . . ." She moved her arms around a bit and then pointed at Salty.

"Wings?" Salty asked.

"Yeah, those. Go slow, and see if anything's wrong with them."

Salty extended one wing and then the other. "They seem okay!"

Aquata took Salty through checking the rest of himself, and at the end they decided that nothing was seriously wrong. He was just a little banged up.

Salty hopped around in excitement, flapping his wings. "This means I can go find my mom!" he cried.

"No, wait!" Ariel held out her hands to stop him. "If you don't know where she is, you should stay here and wait for her to find you."

Andrina pulled herself up to sit on the other side of Ariel. "She's right. You'll only get more lost if you just fly around looking."

"But what if she . . . What if I . . ." Salty trailed off and then made a frustrated noise. "I don't want to be lost anymore!"

"We know how you feel," Ariel said.

"Do we ever!" added Andrina.

"We'll wait with you," said Aquata. Then she stretched out on the rock and dozed off. Ariel and Andrina told Salty all about their adventure so far. Just as they were getting to the end of the story, they heard a new voice.

"Salty! Saaaaaaaaaall-teeeeeeee!"

"Mom!" Salty shouted happily.

Ariel and Andrina watched as Salty flew toward a much larger bird who had appeared above them. The two seagulls danced around each other, squawking their greetings. Together they swooped back down to the island.

"Mom, look—I told you!" Salty said as they landed. "Mermaids! The wave made them lost, too! They said they couldn't see with the water all mucky, so they had to come up, and then they found me!"

"I don't believe it!" said the mother seagull. "I just do not believe it. I haven't seen mermaids around these parts—around any parts—in years. Oh! Where are my manners? Salty says you've been looking after him. I just can't thank you enough."

"You're very wel—" Ariel started to say.

"My, my!" the mother went on as if Ariel hadn't spoken. "That wave certainly was a big one, wasn't it? I keep telling Salty here,

'You have to be ready to dodge waves,' but that one was enormous! Have you ever seen anything like it?"

"No, never. I—" Ariel began.

"And when it hit Salty!" the mother interrupted again. "Oh my goodness me, it just swept him right out of the air, and I did *not* know where he had gone! I was so worried!" She reached out a wing and pulled Salty close to her, nuzzling his head.

"Mom!" Salty whined. "You're messing up my feathers!"

"Your feathers will just have to deal with it," his mother replied. Then she seemed to notice Aquata for the first time. "Is this one all right?" she asked, hopping over to peer at the mermaid's sleeping face. "I'm Sunny," she said, nudging Aquata with one foot. "Hello?"

Aquata opened her eyes sleepily and—

"*Aaaaaaah!*" she shrieked.

Both seagulls took off in alarm, hovering a few feet above the rock. "She seems fine," said Sunny after a moment.

"Aquata, it's okay!" Ariel said. "This is Salty's mom, Sunny. She found him!"

"Yes, oh my, yes, I lost my son and I found my son and I met three lovely young mermaids. It *has* been quite the day. All before lunchtime!" Sunny flitted back down to the rock again. "My sister is never going to believe this. She's always telling me the wildest stories. Why, just last week she told me about these funny little fish. They live so deep underwater, where it's always dark, she said, and they have patches on their faces that light up! Can you imagine? And they talk by blinking their patches at one another! Can you *imagine*? Now, *those* little darlings would have come in handy in that muck, I bet! My sister said she heard about them from some dolphins, who heard about them from . . . Well, I forget who they heard about them from. But now do I have a story for *her*! Mermaids! My goodness."

When Sunny paused to breathe, Ariel jumped in. "You said you had seen mermaids before."

"Why, yes, but not for years now," Sunny replied.

"Do you remember where you saw them?" Ariel asked.

"It was in a little cove, that way," said Sunny, pointing with her wing.

"And is that the same direction the wave came from?"

"Well, now that you mention it, yes, it is!" Sunny responded.

"Then we need to go that way to get home!" Ariel decided, turning to her sisters.

"In that case, I'm afraid you've got quite a journey ahead of you," Sunny said. "That cove is a ways off."

"Oh no," Aquata groaned. "I'm still so tired. Just the thought of a long swim is making my tail hurt."

"Speaking of dolphins . . . ," Sunny began, then flapped away, Salty close behind her. The mermaids quickly lost sight of them.

"We were speaking of dolphins?" asked Andrina into the stunned silence that followed.

"That was so strange," grumbled Aquata.

"Well, it looks like it's just us again now. Let's see if the water's clear enough to—"

"Ta-da!" yelled Sunny, flying back into view.

Ariel, Aquata, and Andrina looked blankly at her.

"I found you some help!" called Sunny. "Come look!"

The three mermaids splashed into the water and saw three dolphins bobbing there, waiting for them.

"I met these fellows when I was looking for Salty," Sunny said, "and they're going your way! Hold on to them and they'll pull you for a while."

"Really?" said Ariel to the closest dolphin. "You don't mind?"

"Not at all," the dolphin said. "It sounds like fun."

"Oh, thank you!" Ariel said. "It *does* sound like fun! And thank *you*," she continued, turning to Salty and his mother.

"No trouble at all," Sunny replied. "It's the least I could do for those who helped my little boy."

"Yeah, thanks!" said Salty. "I hope you get home soon! Bye!"

"Good-bye!" the three mermaids called after them, and the friendly seagulls once again flapped out of sight.

Chapter 5
Swimming Toward Danger

The mermaids had such a good time with their new dolphin friends that they almost forgot they were lost. The girls held tight to the fins on the dolphins' backs while the dolphins skipped along the water and splashed through the waves. Sometimes the dolphins raced one another as the girls cheered them on. Before they knew it, the rocky island disappeared behind them, and soon the dolphins slowed until they were floating along calmly.

"This is as far as we're going in your direction," said the dolphin Ariel was riding. "You can't see the cove yet, but it's not too much farther. Just keep heading this way."

"Thank you again," Ariel said, hugging the dolphin's broad back. "You've made our journey so much easier, and fun, too!"

"I'll say," Andrina agreed.

"Come visit Atlantica sometime!" added Aquata. "When I'm rested up, I bet I could beat all three of you in a race."

The dolphins chuckled, then jumped in the air to wave good-bye.

"Well," Aquata said to Ariel once the dolphins had swum off, "what do you think?"

"I think that was the most fun I've had in ages!" Ariel replied. "I think dolphins are wonderful, and I think the sun feels so good on my face, and I think I'd like to meet Salty's aunt someday."

Aquata laughed. "No, silly," she said. "I mean, what do you think we should do now?"

Ariel stared. "You're asking me?"

Andrina tousled Ariel's hair playfully. "Yeah, we're asking you, little sis. You're on a roll today."

"No kidding," said Aquata. "I'll be

honest, I never would have talked to that seagull."

"Me either," Andrina said. "Not in a million years. And it worked out great! So what do you think?"

Ariel thought for a moment. "Well, now that we're closer to home, we could dive down and ask for directions."

"All right," said Aquata. "Let's give it a shot. And maybe we can find something to eat while we're at it. Breakfast was a long time ago!"

Ariel grinned as she and her sisters dove down into the clear blue water. She had felt confident since they'd gotten to the surface, but now she felt confident *and* smart. This day was turning out to be— *Wait, what is that?* A hulking shape came into view below them. It didn't look like a rock or plant, and it definitely wasn't alive. *Is that...?*

"Ariel, stop!" Aquata grabbed her by the arm. "That's a shipwreck!"

"Whoa!" Ariel whispered. She had heard all about shipwrecks; they were one of Andrina's favorite subjects for a spooky bedtime story. But Ariel had never seen one up close before.

"Oh no, here we go," muttered Andrina.

"What do you mean, 'here we go'?" Aquata said, still holding Ariel back. "We are not going anywhere near that thing! It's dangerous and full of human stuff! Look over there." She motioned to one side of the wreck, where a lovely little coral reef had formed on a shelf of rocks. "We can get directions there."

As the girls swam toward the reef, Ariel found that she couldn't take her eyes off the ship. *It's just as scary as I imagined,* she thought. *I wonder what the inside looks like! Not that I want to go in there, but . . .* "Full of human stuff"? *I wonder what kind of stuff?*

It was oddly quiet among the coral. When the sisters played by the reef near home, there were always plenty of sea creatures around, darting in and out of the coral and sponges. But here there was no sign of anyone.

"Hello?" Aquata called. "Hello?"

"Shhhh!" came a hiss.

The girls froze. Ariel peered around more closely. Where had the voice come from? She couldn't see anyone.

Very quietly, Ariel spoke. "Hello there. We didn't mean to be loud."

Silence.

Ariel continued, just as softly, "We're lost, and we need some help."

Silence.

"Please?" she added.

Another silence, long enough that Ariel almost tried again. Then the sound came louder; it was a sea creature in the coral. *"Shhhh! Hide!"*

The girls looked around in alarm. "Hide from what?" Andrina asked.

A shadow fell over them, and they looked up and gasped.

Sharks!

Chapter 6
The Great White Escape

Ariel moved quickly. "Come on!" she whispered to her sisters.

The sharks were gliding overhead. It seemed that they hadn't noticed the girls yet. Ariel and her sisters still had time to hide. But there was nowhere big enough for them on the reef. Ariel headed to the only other place: the shipwreck.

She felt a hand catch her tail from behind and looked back to see Aquata, her eyes huge with alarm, shaking her head. Ariel turned to Andrina, who nodded. They reached for Aquata, and the three of them made their way toward the wreck.

Soon enough, the ship hovered over them. Ariel spotted a jagged hole in the side, just above the seafloor. She pointed, and the three of them swam carefully through it. They stopped just inside, clutching the edges of the opening and peeking at the sharks above.

Ariel looked nervously over her shoulder

at the inside of the wreck. *Well,* she thought, *I wanted to know what it looked like in here. It seems pretty quiet so far.*

In the light that filtered through the hole, she could make out a small room. The ship had sunk crookedly into the sea, so the walls rose at an angle to a low ceiling, now hung with seaweed. The floor sloped away beneath them, and in the farthest, lowest corner of the room, Ariel saw large shadows in a heap.

She glanced back out of the hole. The sharks still swam lazily, but they were getting farther away. *We're lucky we swam down from the surface when we did,* Ariel realized. *We just missed them!*

Next to her, Aquata breathed a sigh of relief. "We're going to be okay," she whispered. "But we should stay here a little while, just to be safe." Then she looked around at the sunken ship and rolled her eyes. "Or at least *safer.*"

Andrina snickered. "Can you imagine Attina's face when we tell her about this? 'And then we decided to hang out in a shipwreck! You know, because it's so *safe!*'"

"Hey, what is this 'we'? This was not my idea!" Aquata said.

"You're right," Andrina replied. "It was Ariel's idea. Again. And it worked. Again. And no human ghosts have eaten us . . . at least, not yet— Ow!" She rubbed her arm where Aquata had just pinched her in irritation.

While her sisters bickered quietly, Ariel made her way to the shadows in the back of the room. *Andrina's right,* she thought. *There are no human ghosts in here. There's nothing to be afraid of. I'll just keep telling myself that. There's nothing to be afraid of.*

Ariel discovered that the shadows were actually a pile of objects. They seemed to be made of the same material as the ship.

Wood, Ariel remembered. *It's called wood.* The objects had hard corners and looked solid and, if Ariel was being honest, not that interesting. But something about the one on top seemed different. Familiar.

Why does this remind me of a clam? Ariel thought. Then she realized that she could open the object, just like a clamshell.

"Ariel!" Aquata whispered from behind her. "What are you doing? Get back here!"

But Ariel wasn't listening. *It opens!* was all she could think. She picked it up. To her surprise, several smaller objects floated out of it! She heard her sisters gasp. Without thinking, she grabbed one. It was a small,

flat circle, also made of wood. On one side, there was a spiky circular decoration. It reminded her of the sun, Ariel decided. She looked up and saw many more wooden circles, some dark and some light, hitting the ceiling above her or getting tangled in the hanging seaweed.

"*Ariel!*" Aquata whispered again.

Ariel tucked the little disk inside her bandeau for safekeeping and then turned to her sisters. "It's okay!" she called softly. "Come look!"

"Are you *kidding* me?" Aquata said. But Andrina's curiosity got the better of her, and she swam over to join Ariel. Together they looked inside the object Ariel had opened.

"There's more stuff in here," Andrina said.

"Yes, *human* stuff, just like I said!" Aquata replied with a huff, floating over to join them. "And we should not be messing around with it! Ariel, put that down!"

Ariel had just picked up something rectangular and heavy. When she got it out, to her surprise, it flopped open in her hands.

The three girls stared down at it. Even Aquata was speechless. They were looking at an image of two humans on a little ship of some kind, barely big enough for the two of them. The humans smiled at each other happily. The sky was blue, the humans wore bright colors, and the ship thing floated along on the peaceful water.

"What *is* this?" Andrina asked, breaking the silence.

"I don't know," Ariel replied, "but it's wonderful."

"Wait," said Aquata. "I think there's more." She pushed at one side of the image, and sure enough, half of it came up and flipped over to reveal another picture, this one of more humans standing on a large green . . . something.

The three sisters crowded close together, wordlessly staring at picture after picture. Ariel couldn't get enough. The humans looked so happy and beautiful, not at all how she'd envisioned them. And there were so many things in the pictures that she didn't understand. She wanted to find out more, but how?

"Ariel!"

"What?" Ariel said, her head jerking up.

"What, what?" Andrina asked.

"Someone called my name," said Ariel.

Aquata wrinkled her nose. "You're hearing things," she decided.

"Aquata!"

Aquata's eyes widened. "Now *I'm* hearing things."

"Andrina!"

The girls stared at one another for a beat; then together they raced for the hole in the side of the ship.

Chapter 7
A Royal Rescue

It was two of King Triton's guards, wearing gold armor and carrying spears! When King Triton had been told the girls were missing, he had sent his guards to search for them. The guards had been out for hours, moving in a widening arc and asking every creature they encountered if they had seen three young mermaids.

The girls were delighted. They were

almost home. And even better, the guards had thought to bring snacks! As the day grew late and the ocean began to dim around them, they made their way toward Atlantica. The sisters alternated between stuffing their mouths and chatting happily with the guards.

"In just a little while, young princesses, you'll be able to see the coral reef where this all started. We're not far now," said the guard captain, a tough mermaid named Tusk. "And a good thing, too. We're losing light."

"I'm sure your father and sisters will be thrilled to see you," added the second guard, a young merman called Gill.

"Oh, our sisters!" cried Ariel. "I was hoping they didn't get caught in the rogue wave, too. Are they all right?"

"They are completely fine," Tusk reassured her. "The wave you spoke of didn't reach them, so you three are the only ones who were swept away."

"Brrr!" Ariel said as she shivered at a sudden cold patch in the water. "That's odd. I wonder where that cold water is coming from."

"Hmm," said Gill. "It seems like we're fighting a current all of a sudden."

Ariel, Aquata, and Andrina looked at

one another in dismay. It couldn't be. But Gill was right: with every passing second, they had to swim harder.

"There shouldn't be a current here. What's happening?" asked Tusk.

"It's another rogue wave," Aquata said, moaning. "What are we going to do?"

"Down!" said Ariel suddenly. "We go down! Quick!" She stopped trying to swim forward and instead dove into the murky waters below her.

"Wait, Princess!" called Gill as the others swam after her. "Where are you going?"

"Our sisters were safe on the reef.

The wave went *over* them," said Ariel, still swimming her hardest. "We have to get *under* this!"

"She's right!" Tusk said from behind her. "Everyone, follow Ariel!"

Ariel could feel the wave pulling at her, but she remembered what Aquata had taught her. *Jump into it,* Ariel thought. She flexed through her back to her tail, over and over. *Whap, whap, whap* went her tail, and down she shot. *I'm doing it!* she realized. *I'm fighting the current by myself!*

The sea grew darker and darker as they dove. "Stay together!" called Tusk.

Ariel looked back over her shoulder. Behind her, Aquata had grabbed hold of Tusk's spear, and Andrina and Gill were holding hands. Ariel shook her head. "Can't slow down yet!" she shouted. "Follow me!"

"We're right behind you!" replied Tusk.

Ariel dove farther into the blackness, and eventually she felt the pull of the wave weaken. *It worked!* she thought.

Suddenly, she clipped her arm on a protruding rock and was spun around. She was too worried about the wave to stop, so she aimed in the direction she thought she'd been going and kept swimming. A few seconds later her outstretched hands banged into another rock formation. *I have to keep going!* Ariel thought, picking a new direction and diving again. Soon she hit another barrier and was knocked back hard, bouncing off more rocks before swirling to a stop in the pitch-darkness.

"Ow!" she cried.

And then there was silence.

"Hello? Tusk? Anyone?"

No answer. Ariel couldn't see a thing in any direction, and she could no longer feel any currents at all.

She was alone and lost in the blackness.

Chapter 8
Lost at Sea

$\mathcal{A}$riel panicked. They had been so close to getting home. There had even been *adults* around. She had been brave and confident and smart and strong, and it hadn't been enough. She was lost again. For all she knew, *everyone* was lost. And she was scared. *I wish I had just stayed home,* she thought, curling into a ball and wrapping her arms around herself. *I wish I had never tried to ride the current. I wish I had never tried anything. If I hadn't tried anything, I'd be safe.*

As she floated in the dark, she felt something under her bandeau. It was the little wooden disk she had found on the ship. Despite her fear, her fingers started tracing the circle. *But if I hadn't tried anything,* she thought, *I'd never have found this. And we'd never have met Salty or the dolphins.*

She remembered Aquata asking her if she was scared to be on the surface, and how good it had felt to realize she hadn't been. She remembered Andrina saying *I'm impressed, little sis.*

She took a deep breath and said "I'm

on a roll" aloud to make herself believe it.

Okay, she thought, *what would someone on a roll do next? I don't know! I don't know where I am. I don't know where anyone else is. I can't see a thing. I can't even tell which way is up!*

Wait. One problem at a time. Just like I told Salty. Let's start with . . . figuring out which way is up. How can I do that in the dark? If it were light out, I'd just swim toward the sun. Oh! Things float up!

She pulled the wooden piece out of her bandeau and made a globe of her hands, trapping the disk inside.

She could feel the wood pushing against her fingers on one side. *Wait, that's up? That can't be right.* She swirled her hands around until the wood wasn't touching any part of her skin, then paused. Again it came to rest against her fingers on the same side.

Whoa, she thought, tilting herself until she was facing the direction the disk had floated. *I got really turned around.* She shuddered, thinking how bad it would have been if she hadn't checked — she'd have swum off in the completely wrong direction!

Next, she thought, *What if I just try going up?*

Carefully, using the feel of the disk against her hands to guide her, she swam upward . . . and almost immediately hit her head on something sharp. She sucked in her breath in pain. Tucking the wooden piece back into her bandeau, she felt above her and discovered a rock ceiling with long stalactites packed closely together.

Ow! she thought. *Just feeling along is not going to work. This would be so much easier if I had some light down here!*

Then she remembered what Salty's mom had said: there were fish in the dark places of the ocean that could make their own light! Salty's mom had described them as "cute" and "little," which sounded all right. But what if there were bigger, meaner fish around?

She thought of the silent reef they had found, how all the creatures had hidden from the sharks among the coral and sponges. *I'll hide up close to the ceiling,* she thought, *and see if I can call any friendly fish to help me. That way, if something big and dangerous comes along, it won't be able to fit between the rocks to get me.*

With this plan in mind, Ariel tucked herself against the ceiling, between a few particularly nasty-feeling stalactites. Then she gathered her courage and called out, "Hello? I'm lost and need help. Hello?"

Nothing happened. She tried again. "I heard there were some fish who might be able to help me. Fish that light up?"

Nothing. *Oh, wait.* "I know you can't talk, and I can't see in the dark, so if you could light up to show me you're here . . ."

Immediately two lights came on, inches from her nose.

Chapter 9
The Dark Tunnels

"Eep!" Ariel yelped before she could stop herself.

The lights went out.

"No, wait!" she said. "I was just startled. Please come back!"

A few feet away, the lights came on briefly and then went out again.

"It's okay," said Ariel. "I'm not going to

hurt you, I promise. I just need some help."

The lights flashed a few times, a bit closer now. In the glow, Ariel could see a small black-and-gray fish. The light came from a half-circle under each of its eyes.

"I'm looking for my sisters and two guards," she told the little fish. "They're all merpeople, like me."

Flash, flash. Flash, flashflashflash, flash—

"Oh no," Ariel said. "I can't understand you. Wait, but—you understand me, right?"

Flash.

"Oh! Does one flash mean yes?"

Flash.

"And how do you say no?"

Flash, flash.

"Okay! So . . . one question at a time. Do you know the way out of here?"

Flash.

"You do! That's wonderful! And have you seen my sisters or the guards?"

Flash, flash.

Ariel's smile disappeared. "Oh."

Flash, flash, flash.

"Wait, what? What does three flashes mean?"

Flash, flash, flash. This time the fish swam much closer to her. *Flash, flash, flash.* Again it swam off.

"Does . . . does three flashes mean to follow you?"

Flash. And then the lights under the fish's eyes came on and stayed on, and she followed the fish out of the stalactites.

The little fish led her to the right, then down, then back to the left. In the glow from its light Ariel could make out rocky passages around them. *Oh,* she thought, *no wonder everything was so confusing. This isn't open water. These are tunnels!*

Eventually the fish stopped. Its lights started flashing rapidly.

"I don't know what that—" Ariel started to say, then stopped as the tunnel around her

lit up with dozens of other lights. "Oh!"

A small school of fish floated in front of her, all with the same lit-up patches under their eyes. The first fish continued its rapid blinking, and a few of the others began blinking in response.

Ariel pointed at the school. "Do they know where my sisters and the guards are?"

Flash.

"Lead the way!" Ariel shouted.

Off they went through the dark tunnels, some of the fish swimming along in front of Ariel while others kept pace with her or spiraled around her as she swam. It was like she was gliding along in her own cloud of lights. *I know there's a lot to be worried about,* thought Ariel, *but this is amazing.*

Then the school moved ahead of her and stopped. Dozens of lights hovered in the blackness in front of her. She waited.

A whimper came from the darkness ahead.

"Aquata, is that you?" Ariel whispered.

"Ariel?" came the reply.

A few of the fish darted forward to cast their lights on Aquata and Tusk, huddled together against a tunnel wall. Tusk held her spear out in front of her, and as the lights approached, she waved it in warning.

Ariel rushed into the space between the spear and the fish. "It's me! These fish are helping!" She hugged Aquata and then turned back to the fish. "Thank you so much. Do you know where the other two merpeople are?"

Flash went the whole school in unison.

Tusk stiffened, and Aquata made a small startled noise.

"That means yes," Ariel said.

Flash, flash, flash.

"And that means we should follow them. Let's go!"

Ariel, Aquata, and Tusk followed the fish to another part of the tunnel, where they found Andrina and Gill carefully feeling their way along a wall. This time Ariel made sure to keep pace with the lead fish so she would be clearly visible.

"Andrina! Gill! It's us!" Ariel called softly to them. Andrina yelped in delight and dove forward to swirl first Ariel and then Aquata around in a huge hug. She was relieved to be reunited with her sisters.

"All right," said Ariel, turning to the school of fish. "We just need one more favor.

Would you show us the way out of these tunnels?"

Flash went the school. *Flash, flash, flash.*

"What the—?" started Andrina.

"One flash means yes," Aquata said. "And three flashes means we can follow them."

"But how—?"

"Ariel figured it out."

Andrina paused, then hugged Ariel again. "Of course she did."

The guards fell in on either side of the three sisters, and together they followed the darting lights out of the tunnels and back into open water.

Chapter 10
The Return to Atlantica

After that, it seemed as if they were back in Atlantica in no time at all. The guards led the girls straight to the palace to see King Triton. Attina, Alana, Adella, and Arista were waiting for them at the arch to the throne room, and they showered the three returning sisters with hugs and kisses.

As they passed through the arch, Ariel

heard Aquata whisper to Adella, "You won't believe what Ariel did. She—"

"Girls!" boomed King Triton from the far end of the room.

Ariel, Aquata, and Andrina glided toward their father. He sat high above them on his elaborate throne, his trident in his hand. As they came closer, he leaned forward to glare at them.

"I am overjoyed that you've returned safely," he said. "But I am also very, very disappointed in you for wandering off in the first place! I'm told you were playing in the current, is that right?"

The girls nodded meekly.

"How many times have I warned you about going too far?" He continued to scowl down at them. "And to go *so* far that you couldn't find your way home again! I thought better of you. Why, if it weren't for the guards, you would have been lost for good!"

Aquata tried to speak up. "But—"

"Guards!" King Triton cut her off. "Come forward."

Tusk and Gill swam up on either side of the three sisters.

"Captain Tusk. Guardsman Gill," King Triton said, nodding to each of them. "I commend your bravery and skill in returning

my daughters to me. You may ask a reward of me in return."

"Your Majesty . . . ," Tusk began. "If I may . . ." She trailed off.

"Continue," said King Triton.

Tusk cleared her throat. "To be honest, the bravery and skill that got us home were not mine or Guardsman Gill's. They were Ariel's."

Triton sat back in surprise. "Proceed."

"We did find them, Your Majesty; it's true," said Tusk. "But shortly afterward, we were about to be caught up in a rogue wave. Ariel's quick thinking saved us from being swept away. She led us down into the deep waters so that the wave would pass over our heads."

Triton raised his eyebrows.

"There's more, Your Majesty," Gill said. "We became separated and lost in a tunnel system, and Ariel found us all in the blackness and led us out."

"Well, the light-up fish did that, really," Ariel said.

"Pardon?" King Triton asked.

"Young Princess Ariel befriended some fish that lit the way for us," Gill explained.

"She also worked out how to communicate with them, Your Majesty, as they don't speak," added Tusk.

"I see," rumbled Triton. "Anything else?"

"As a matter of fact, yes, Your Majesty," Tusk said. "It's worth noting that, when we found the young princesses, they were well on their way to returning home all by themselves."

King Triton turned to Aquata. "Is this true?" he asked her.

Aquata took a deep breath to steady her nerves. "Well, first, we didn't just wander off. There was a rogue wave over the reef this morning, like the one that almost caught us and the guards this afternoon. Only, we didn't know what it was at the time, so we didn't know how to get away from it, and it took us far away, and—"

"One moment, Aquata," Triton interrupted. He called over one of his advisers. "Two rogue waves in the area in one day? Take the workmen out tomorrow and see about building new breakwaters near the reef. That should make things safer."

He turned back to the girls. "It seems I must apologize. I thought you had been careless, when in fact you've been incredibly unlucky."

Andrina cleared her throat.

King Triton raised an eyebrow, amused. "Yes, Andrina?"

"Aquata's the one who pulled us out of the wave. Without her, we'd have been even farther away," said Andrina.

"Only because I was the biggest," Aquata said.

"And the *strongest*," Ariel put in, nudging her sister.

"But then Aquata was really tired," Andrina continued, "and Ariel took over!"

"Oh," said Ariel, embarrassed. "I didn't think of it like—"

"Shush, little sis," Andrina interrupted. She turned back to King Triton. "Ariel had all these great ideas, and they helped us get closer to home. We might still be lost without her."

King Triton thought for a moment. "I must apologize again. I said I was disappointed in you, but in fact I am quite the opposite. You girls have been very resourceful, and I am proud and at ease knowing that you can take care of yourselves in a crisis."

Then he turned to Ariel. "And Captain Tusk was right. You deserve special praise for the bravery and skill you displayed today. What would you like as your reward?"

In that moment, Ariel felt just as

confident and smart and strong as she had ever hoped to be. And she knew exactly what she wanted for a reward. "After breakfast tomorrow, will you come play with us on the reef?"

King Triton laughed. "There is nothing I'd like more."

Chapter 11
Mermaid Talk

After the king dismissed them, the seven sisters rushed to their bedroom to talk.

"I can't believe this!" Arista started as soon as they got through the doorway. "If I had taken that last ride in the current, I'd have gotten swept away, too! Ugh, there is no way I would have wanted to be lost in those tunnels."

"You haven't heard the half of it," Andrina said, flopping down on her bed.

"What do you mean?" asked Alana.

Andrina just smirked, and Aquata started laughing.

"What?" asked Adella, bobbing with excitement. *What? Tell us!*"

Andrina couldn't draw the suspense out any longer. She leaned forward and whispered so that no one passing by the bedroom would hear. "We went . . . to the surface."

"*What?*" Adella shrieked. Alana clapped her hands over her mouth.

Arista darted over to sit on the edge of Andrina's bed. "Are you serious?" she asked, looking nervous. "Do you know what Daddy would do if he knew?"

Aquata shrugged. "We didn't have a choice. And anyway, it wasn't so bad. It was actually . . . fun."

Arista raised an eyebrow. "Fun? Fun how?"

Crossing her arms, Attina frowned. "Let's not get any ideas, all right?"

"But, Attina," Arista protested, "we *have* to hear the story!"

Aquata laughed. "Well, after I pulled us out of the wave, the water was all mucky.

Ariel swam us up to the surface, just so we could see. And then she— Wait, Ariel, you should tell this part. Ariel?"

The sisters turned to find Ariel gazing out the bedroom window.

"Ariel?" Aquata said again. "Do you want to tell about meeting the bird?"

"You met a *bird*?" Adella squealed. Alana advanced on her again, and Adella clapped her own hands over her mouth this time.

Attina went to where Ariel was still looking out the window. "Ariel?" she asked. "Are you all right? What's on your mind?"

Ariel pointed to the bright-red sponges just outside. "It's those sponges. I've been

thinking about where they came from, and . . . Did you know there's part of our reef that we've never explored?"

Attina was surprised at the change in topic. "What?" was all she could muster.

Encouraged, Ariel went on. "It's true! I saw it on the way home with the guards. It's just beyond a little shelf we don't usually pass. We have some time before dinner. . . . I bet we could find more sponges like this. And I think I saw a cave!"

Aquata's mouth dropped open. "You

can't be serious," she said. "Haven't you had enough adventure for one day?"

"No kidding," Andrina added. "I mean, between the birds and the dolphins and the sharks—"

"*Mmmmmph!*" Adella squeaked from behind her hands.

"And the shipwreck—"

Attina gasped. "What about a shipwreck?"

"And those human pictures! We still haven't told them about the pictures!"

"You are absolutely *killing* me with this," Arista moaned, throwing herself backward onto Andrina's bed. "What pictures?"

"Oh! That reminds me," Aquata said

to Ariel. "You never told us what you were thinking when you went poking around in all that stuff in the ship. How did you know that . . . thing even opened like that?"

Ariel thought about it. "It reminded me of a clam," she said. "And there were more of them that we didn't open. Next time I'll bring—"

"*Next time?*" Attina interrupted, her eyes widening.

"Um," Ariel mumbled, shrinking back. "Well, let's go out to the reef!" She pushed away from the window.

"Ariel . . . ," Attina said.

Ariel was swimming out of the room.

She stopped at the doorway and turned back to her sisters. "Come on!" she called. "If you go to the reef with me, I'll tell you all about the human pictures!"

Adella followed her first. "And the bird, please!"

Alana went next. "Did you say something about dolphins?"

Then Arista. "And sharks! I definitely heard the word *sharks*!"

Attina followed, sighing. "I'd better go keep an eye on her."

Then it was just Aquata and Andrina alone in the bedroom. Andrina looked over at her sister, a sparkle in her eye. "If she finds a cave . . ."

Aquata finished the thought. "I do *not* want to miss it!"

And then the two of them were out the door, laughing and calling, "Ariel! Wait up!"